MW00899549

Eldridge the Scaredy Red Balloon

Anthony Canonica

Copyright © 2021 Anthony Canonica
All rights reserved
First Edition

Fulton Books, Inc.
Meadville, PA

Published by Fulton Books 2021

ISBN 978-1-64952-318-1 (paperback)
ISBN 978-1-63985-188-1 (hardcover)
ISBN 978-1-64952-319-8 (digital)

Printed in the United States of America

For Luca Canonica, the newest addition to a family of doers

Eldridge the red balloon lived at Hector's Party Store on Third Street, right between The Pet Shop and the Bargain Hut.

Outside the window Eldridge could see birds singing in the trees, kids playing in the street, and planes flying in the sky, but Eldridge never participated in any of those things. You see, Eldridge was scared.

Eldridge was afraid of being popped, dropped, bumped, thumped, scraped, and scratched; but more than anything, Eldridge was afraid of heights.

All the other balloons could not wait to be purchased and enjoy a birthday party, attend a wedding, or welcome a new baby into the world. After all, balloons were made for celebrations; the possibilities were endless.

But Eldridge didn't share the enthusiasm of his fellow balloons. Eldridge loved the comfort of Hector's Party Store; perhaps what he liked most was the predictability. Every day the store opened at six and closed at nine. The confetti was always next to the whistles and across from the costumes. Every day was exactly as the last.

Except, this day was different. It started just as any other, but everything changed when a family walked through Hector's door. Eldridge could see a young boy walking toward him. The small boy violently grabbed Eldridge by his string and yanked him across the store. Eldridge bopped and banged against the store's shelves as the boy aggressively advanced toward his mother and father.

The boy grunted and barked at his parents, "I want this balloon! You better buy this for me! I want this balloon!"

At this point, the child was in hysterics. He beat his head and arms against the floor until the color of the boy's face matched Eldridge's shiny red rubber body. In a moment of weakness, the parents agreed to purchase the balloon just to end their son's tantrum. As the family headed out the door, red balloon in hand, Eldridge went into a state of panic.

"What's happening? Don't let them take me outside!"

In all his excitement, the little boy carelessly let go of Eldridge's string on the way to the car.

"Oh no! Please, someone help me!"

Eldridge flew higher and higher, only to be stopped momentarily by briefly brushing a rough tree branch. As Eldridge soared through the clouds, he could see his old home at the party store, but beyond that, he saw the entire town! He could see the city hall and the library. He saw the park, the grocery store, and places he never even imagined. Everyone stood and stared as Eldridge climbed through the sky. For once, everyone was looking at him.

In that moment, Eldridge realized that life was not something to be feared, but something to be experienced. Eldridge traveled the world, seeing all the greatest monuments around the globe.

He marveled at the lights in New York City, listened to the music of Spain, and could smell the food in Italy.

He tasted the salt in the air off the beaches of Brazil and could feel the warmth between two lovers walking in France.

Eldridge knew that if he never left the comfort of Hector's Party Store, he would have never seen all these amazing things. He learned that it's okay to feel scared but, sometimes, the most rewarding things in life are just one step outside your comfort zone.

While Eldridge was exploring the world; he passed by a friendly blue jay.

"What are you doing all the way up here?" asked the blue jay. "Balloons are supposed to be at birthday parties!"

"Oh, I feel like I'm at a party! But I would like to go home now."

The blue jay carried Eldridge back down to Hector's Party Store and promised to pick Eldridge up any time he was ready to go on a journey.

By the end of his adventures, Eldridge no longer was afraid of being popped, dropped, bumped, thumped, scraped, or scratched; and most importantly, Eldridge lost his fear of heights and allowed himself to embrace all the joys the world had to offer.

About the Author

Eldridge the Scaredy Red Balloon is Anthony Canonica's first published book, but he is no stranger to trying new things and learning new skills—from sanitation worker to lifeguard, from educator to Broadway wigmaker and reality TV contestant. Anthony now makes a living as a special effects makeup artist in film and television and has aspirations to open his own restaurant. Anthony recollects, "One day while working in Manhattan, I noticed a single balloon going beyond the highest skyscraper, and my first thought was, 'How funny would it be if a balloon was afraid of heights?' But then I thought, I bet a lot of people can relate to that feeling, allowing the fear of failure to control their lives." Anthony encourages everyone to allow themselves to feel fear, but then proceed anyway, because if you spend your time pursuing what you love, take a lot of calculated risks, and manage expectation, success and happiness is inevitable.

CPSIA information can be obtained
at www.ICGtesting.com
Printed in the USA
BVHW021756290821
615541BV00005B/172

9 781639 851881